CLARK THE SHARK
DARES TO SHARE

WRITTEN BY BRUCE HALE   ILLUSTRATED BY GUY FRANCIS

HARPER

An Imprint of HarperCollinsPublishers

To Charlie and Oliver
—B.H.

For Lewis, Alyssa, Jack, and Poppy
—G.F.

Clark the Shark Dares to Share
Copyright © 2014 by HarperCollins Publishers
All rights reserved. Manufactured in China.
No part of this book may be used or reproduced in any manner whatsoever without
written permission except in the case of brief quotations embodied in critical articles
and reviews. For information address HarperCollins Children's Books, a division of
HarperCollins Publishers, 10 East 53rd Street, New York, NY 10022.
www.harpercollinschildrens.com

ISBN 978-0-06-227905-7

13 14 15 16 17   SCP   10 9 8 7 6 5 4 3 2 1
❖
First Edition

Clark the Shark loved school! He loved his teacher and he loved learning. But sometimes Clark got a little mixed-up. One marvelous morning Mrs. Inkydink told Clark's class, "Time for Show and Share!"

History
Math
Oceanography
Recess

Benny Blowfish went first. He played a song so sweet and sassy that Clark couldn't help but dance his Funky Shark dance—with a *hip*, and a *hop*, and a *skiddly-widdly-wop!*

"Sit down, please!" said Mrs. Inkydink.

"But I was sharing too!" said Clark.

"Sharing is caring," said Mrs. Inkydink. "And everyone must learn to wait their turn."

"I get it," said Clark. But he didn't really.

At Reading Roundup, Amanda Eelwiggle
won a scrumptious prize for reading the most books.

"Sea slug ice cream?" asked Clark.

"Yum yum, I want some!"

"That's up to Amanda," said Mrs. Inkydink.

"But sharing is caring!"
cried Clark.

Mrs. Inkydink nodded. "Yes, I'm aware.
But the *giver* chooses when to share."

"Sharing is confusing," said Clark.

In reef hockey, Clark chose to share his spectacular skills.

"HOCKEY IS AWESOME!"
he roared.

Clark front faked and back faked; he stick checked and deked.

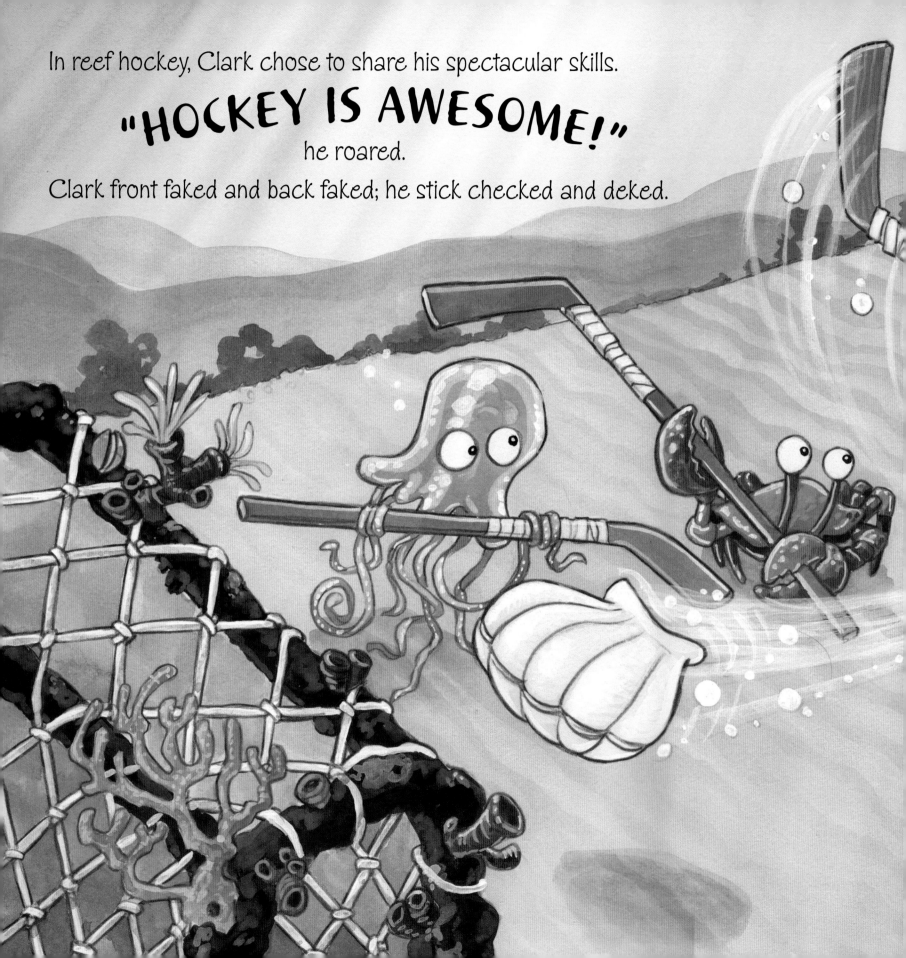

In the end, Clark did everything but pass the puck. His teammates were cranky.

"Hey, hotshot. Let someone else score, why don't you?" said his best friend, Joey Mackerel.

"But we all shared the win," said Clark.

Coach Crabby scowled. "A win's not okay unless we all get to play."

"Sharing is complicated," said Clark.

After school, Clark and Joey Mackerel played Sea Wars at Joey's house.

"Wow, is that Dark Wader?" asked Clark.

"Best birthday present ever," said Joey. "Wanna play with Fluke Seawalker?"

Clark *reeeally* wanted Dark Wader, but Joey asked him to wait his turn.

Then, when Joey went to get them a snack, Clark couldn't resist.

"Must be my turn!"

It was, after all, the coolest toy ever.

"SEA WARS ROCKS!"
cried Clark.

POW!

BAM!

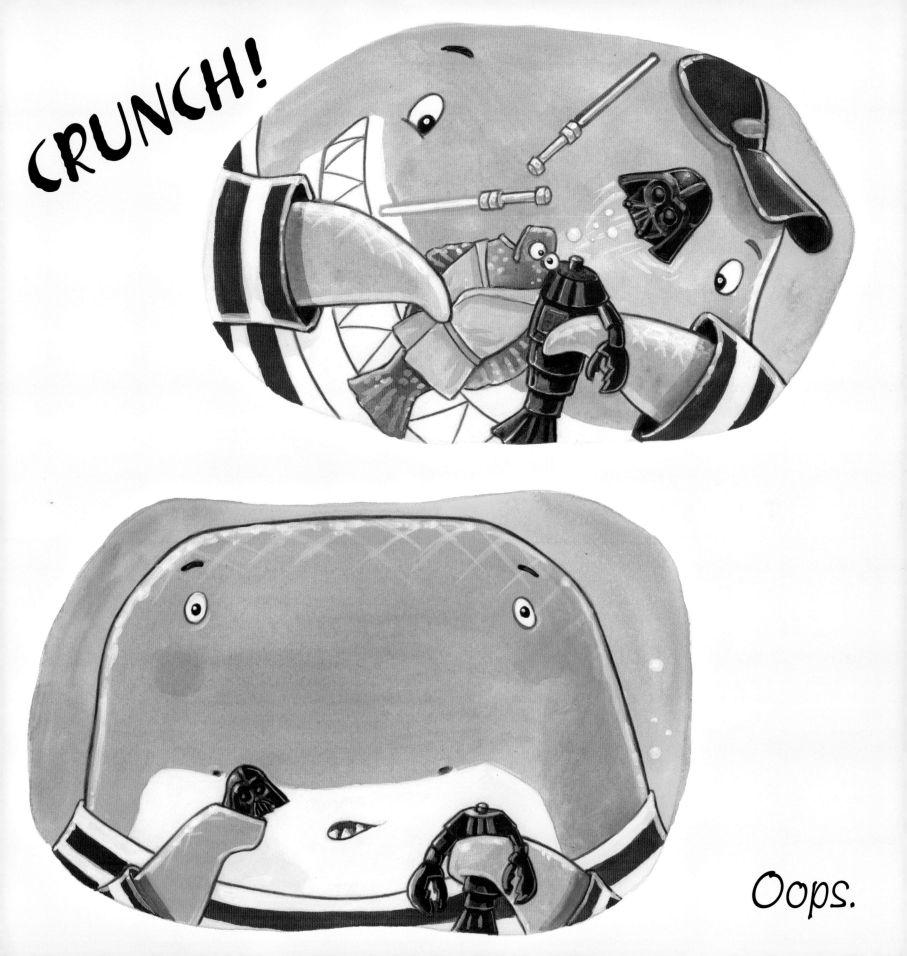

"Clark!" cried Joey. "You broke it!"

"Sorry," said Clark. "I was . . . sharing?"

Joey shook his head. "That's not sharing," he said. "That's taking and breaking."

Clark the Shark swam home befuddled and bewildered.
He didn't understand sharing at *all*.

And when he arrived, Clark found he wasn't the only one who didn't get it.

"Mom!" cried Clark. "My cap! He borrowed it, he bit it, and now it's *ruined*."

"Teething or no teething," Clark's mother said, "that's no way to treat a cap."

She told his brother to ask before borrowing, but she told Clark, "You have heaps of caps. And if you have a lot, why not share a lot?"

But Clark didn't want to hear it. He swam to his room and sulked up a storm.

"Sharing is caring," Clark grumbled. "It's not taking and breaking."

But this only reminded him of what he'd done at Joey's house. Clark's head hurt, as if a big, sharky thought was trying to break free.

"So, sharing is . . . waiting your turn, letting everyone play, the giver chooses when, not taking and breaking, *and* giving what you've got a lot of?"

Sharing *was* confusing.

But, thought Clark, it also might be worth getting right.

"Mom," he asked, "will you help me bake something?"

The next day, Clark gave Joey a home-baked krill cake and a great big sharky apology.

"I think I'll share this with the whole class," said Joey.

"Really?" said Clark.

"Really," said Joey.

And when Amanda Eelwiggle saw all that cake being cut up,
she said, "You know what goes well with krill cake?"

"No, what?" said Clark.

"Sea slug ice cream!"

And just like that, she scooped her treat onto everyone's plates.

Clark the Shark looked around at all his classmates enjoying cake and ice cream and he got a warm, wiggly feeling way down deep inside.

"What is it, Clark?" asked Mrs. Inkydink.

With a gi-normous grin, Clark broke into the funkiest, sharkiest Funky Shark dance ever. And this time, all his classmates joined him— with a *hip*, and a *hop*, and a *skiddly-widdly-wop!*

"SHARING IS SWEET!"

cried Clark the Shark.